Finding Monkey Moon

ELIZABETH PULFORD

illustrated by

KATE WILKINSON

CANDLEWICK PRESS

Every night at half past seven,
Michael and Monkey Moon
went *hippity-hop, hippity-hop*
up the stairs to bed.

But one night when Michael said,
"Come on, Monkey Moon.
It's time to go," Monkey Moon
couldn't be found in any of
his favorite places.

He wasn't hiding under the sofa.
He wasn't tucked behind a chair.

He wasn't playing in the toy box.
"He must be at the park," said Dad.

So Michael pulled on his jacket,
his rain boots, and hat.
He opened the back door
and stepped outside into the
big, dark night.

"It's all right, Monkey Moon!"
he yelled. "I'm coming
to get you."

"Hey," said Dad. "Wait for me."

Together they walked down the quiet street,
their breath fluttering like moths in the cold air.

"Don't be scared, Monkey Moon," Michael cried.

"I'm coming."

An owl gave a soft *hoot, hoot*,

and Michael moved closer to Dad.

Leaves scuffed around their feet as they walked.

"It won't be long now, Monkey Moon!" shouted Michael.

Dad bent down and scooped up Michael.
He swung him high onto his shoulders
and said, "There you go, young fella."

Deeper and deeper into the park
they went.

Past the silent swings. Past the
duck pond and the sleeping ducks.

"Where are you, Monkey Moon?"
Michael called out.

On and on they went . . .

behind the closed-up popcorn truck and
under the archway that led to the picnic area.

"I'm here, Monkey Moon. Where are you?"
said Michael, brushing away a pile of rotting leaves.
But there was only the prickly bump of a
snoozing hedgehog.

"Are you here?" said Michael, lifting up the large, flat
leaf of a plant. But there was only the sound of
a small animal scurrying away.

Michael ran over to the tall trees.

He peered behind each one.

But there was no Monkey Moon.

Michael looked under the old wooden bench.

He searched the sandbox and inside the little playhouse.

He jumped down the few steps into
the sunken garden—all the time crying,
"Monkey Moon! Monkey Moon!
Where are you?"

But every time there was only a big,
black silence in return.

Michael's lips trembled.
Where was Monkey Moon?
What had happened to him?

He put his hands to his mouth
and shouted as loud as he could,
one last time. "Monkey Moon!"

His cry carried through the darkness
and fell into the folds of quiet,
but still there wasn't a single sound,
not even the tiniest whisper.

"Monkey Moon's gone,"
he said to Dad.

Michael kicked out at the nearby bush, making
the branches shimmer and shift for a few seconds.

But wait. What was that? It looked like
a shiny eye winking at him.

"Oh, Monkey Moon," he said. "There you are."

Michael picked up Monkey Moon and hugged him close. "Now you don't have to be frightened anymore."

Michael swung Monkey Moon high onto his shoulders and said, "There you go, young fella."

And with that, the three of them headed home, Michael and Monkey Moon going *hippity-hop*, *hippity-hop* all the way.

For Fraser John and our girls, Francesca and Scarlett. x

K. W.

First U.S. edition 2015

Library of Congress Catalog Card Number 2012950627
ISBN 978-0-7636-6777-1

15 16 17 18 19 20 CCP 10 9 8 7 6 5 4 3 2 1

Printed in Shenzhen, Guangdong, China

This book was typeset in Integrity.
The illustrations were done in acrylic.

Candlewick Press
99 Dover Street
Somerville, Massachusetts 02144

visit us at www.candlewick.com